# THE FAMOUS FIVE AND THE GOLDEN GALLEON

THE FAMOUS FIVE are Julian, Dick, George (Georgina by rights), Anne and Timmy the dog.

A wrecked yacht, *The Golden Galleon*, is washed up near Kirrin Island, with a cargo of gold ingots. The five discover it was used by some bank robbers for their get-away, and when the gold vanished overnight the Five embark on an exciting treasure hunt.

**Also available in Knight Books:**

# The Famous Five And The Golden Galleon

A new adventure of the characters created by Enid Blyton, told by Claude Voilier, translated by Anthea Bell

*Illustrated by John Cooper*

**KNIGHT BOOKS**
Hodder and Stoughton

Copyright © Librairie Hachette 1974
First published in France as *Les Cinq et le Galion D'Or*
English language translation copyright
Hodder & Stoughton Ltd. 1982
Illustrations copyright © Hodder & Stoughton Ltd. 1982

*First published in Great Britain by Knight Books 1982*

**British Library C.I.P.**

Voilier, Claude
  The Famous Five and the golden galleon. –
  (Knight books)
  I. Title    II. Les Cinq et le galion d'or. *English*
  843'.914[J]       PZ7

ISBN 0-340-27866-8

---

Printed and bound in Great Britain for
Hodder and Stoughton Paperbacks, a
division of Hodder and Stoughton Ltd.,
Mill Road, Dunton Green, Sevenoaks,
Kent (Editorial Office: 47 Bedford
Square, London WC1 3DP) by
Hunt Barnard Printing Ltd.,
Aylesbury, Bucks.

# CONTENTS

## Chapter One

## ON KIRRIN ISLAND AGAIN

'Come on, Dick, do get the boat untied! Help him push it out, Julian! Anne, you have a last look at our camping equipment to make sure we haven't forgotten anything! As for you, Timmy, can't you stop going round and round chasing your tail like that? It's still just where you left it!'

'Yes, *sir*!' said Dick, saluting smartly.

'Aye, aye, cap'n!' said Julian, standing to attention.

'All right, George,' agreed Anne, counting the parcels standing round her for the third time.

'Woof!' said Timmy, and he actually did stop going round and round like a whirling dervish.

George scowled, feeling partly annoyed by the way her cousins were laughing at her and partly as though she'd like to laugh herself! George might have a quick temper, but she had a good sense of humour too.

Just at the moment she was really very happy. She and her cousins were going to spend the summer holidays together, as they did every year. The children called themselves the Five – the fifth of them was Timmy, George's dog, who was quite inseparable from her. The Five came across all sorts of puzzling mysteries, and they loved solving them. They hoped something exciting was going to happen to them these holidays too.

Just now, however, the Five were busy thinking about the fun they were going to have on Kirrin Island. They were going to camp out there like Robinson Crusoe – that would be a good adventure in itself!

George's parents, Uncle Quentin and Aunt Fanny, lived by the sea in Kirrin Cottage, close to the little village of Kirrin. The garden of Kirrin Cottage went down to the beach, and George's rowing boat was tied up there.

'Ready to put to sea, cap'n!' announced Dick solemnly.

'Mustn't keep George waiting!' agreed Julian, who hadn't taken long to untie the boat from its moorings.

'I really do *believe* we've got everything, George,' said Anne seriously, putting the list she had been consulting back in her pocket.

George did start laughing then.

'All right, I know you all think I'm funny!' she

said. 'But I don't mind! We're going to camp on Kirrin Island – oh, won't it be fun? I feel as if I was leading a real explorer's expedition!'

With her short curly hair, tanned legs and blue shorts, George looked more like a boy than a girl. Dick, who was eleven, the same age as his cousin, was very like her. They both had bright eyes and dark hair, and they were both very lively and impulsive.

Julian was thirteen. He was the eldest of the four cousins, and he and Anne, the youngest – she was ten – were more sensible. They were both fair-haired, and they were the ones who calmed the other two down a bit.

As for Timmy, the fifth of the Five, he was no ordinary dog! Perhaps it wouldn't have been a good idea to ask about his ancestry – but he was very intelligent, and he had a wonderful nose for picking up a scent. He adored George and followed her about like a shadow. His little mistress knew she could always count on Timmy to be brave, devoted and very faithful.

'Come on, then, all push together, and we're off to sea!'

George couldn't have been more enthusiastic if she had really been the captain of a pirate ship about to board another vessel!

'Hey, just a minute!' protested Julian. 'Give us a chance to get our camping things on board first!'

George went red. Though she usually took the

lead when the four cousins were together, she did get carried away, and needed Julian to bring her down to earth sometimes.

Laughing and splashing and pretending to squabble, the children ran the boat out into the water, and soon they were all on board. George and Dick took the oars and started rowing towards Kirrin Island.

Believe it or not, Kirrin Island really did belong to George. Her parents had given it to her for her very own. It was not a very big island, just a piece of land which had got cut off from the mainland by the sea thousands and thousands of years ago, but the children thought it was a wonderful place. It was very picturesque and mysterious, and it had everything you could want on an island: a little cove, well sheltered from the wind, which made a natural harbour, a sandy beach, rocks, a spring of pure water, grass, big trees – and even a ruined old castle, with its walls still standing. They towered above the sea.

As George rowed she was telling herself how lucky she was to own her island. Over on Kirrin Island, you felt quite cut off from the rest of the world!

'Watch out, George, you're day-dreaming!' Dick suddenly said. 'You're sending us all over the place, old girl! Keep the boat steady!'

George cast her cousin a withering glance. If there was one thing she hated it was being called

Soon they were all aboard, and rowing towards Kirrin Island.

When the tents were up, George and Dick went to fetch water from the spring.

a girl, or having people use her real name, Georgina. She did so wish she had been born a boy instead! Unlike Anne, she hated sewing, cooking and doing housework. She liked boisterous games instead, and she was so bold that she sometimes even alarmed her cousin Dick.

'It's all right,' she said crossly, but she struck out hard with her oar to get the boat back on course.

A few more strokes, and the boat entered the island's sheltered little inlet. With shouts of delight, Julian, Dick and George jumped into the shallow water and drew the boat up. They tied it to an iron ring fixed into a rock.

Anne got out of the boat too. Timmy was already rolling about on the sand, barking happily.

'Let's hurry to get out things up the path,' Julian suggested. 'Then I'll pull the boat right up onto the beach. It looks as if the weather's set fair, but you never know – and we don't want to risk leaving the boat where it might get driven on the rocks!'

Julian was right, it really was lovely weather. It was still quite early in the morning, but the sun was already shining brightly in a cloudless blue sky.

'Come on, then! Got the tents, Ju? Dick, you carry the tent pegs, and I'll bring the inflatable mattresses. If those cooking things are too heavy for you, Anne, just leave them and we'll come back for them later.'

'We'll have to come back anyway, to fetch the stove and the provisions,' Julian pointed out. 'Don't get so worked up, George! There's no hurry!'

The path which led from the cove up to the low hill overlooking the sea was quite a steep, hard climb. But the children had good strong legs and were sure-footed. As for Timmy he could go faster than any of them with his four paws. Of course, as Anne remarked, it was true that Timmy didn't have anything to carry!

George was chattering away and dancing about excitedly. She just couldn't help it – she so loved coming to camp on Kirrin Island. This was one place she could shout and sing as much as she liked, without having to worry about disturbing her father's important scientific work! Uncle Quentin was rather strict, and liked to have peace and quiet.

'You know,' she told the others, 'Kirrin Island is really the perfect place for us to go when we want to be all on our own, without any grown – ups to bother us!'

Once they had reached the grassy space where they were going to camp, in front of the old castle, the children put their things down and started pitching two good-sized tents, one for the girls and the other for the boys. There was a third tent, too, a little square one, to hold the stove and the provisions. The food was kept in a safe, so that no nasty insects could get at it.

When the tents were up and securely fastened in place, Julian went back down to the cove and pulled the boat well in, away from the rocks. George and Dick went to fetch water from the spring, and Anne started getting lunch. While she was busy with her saucepans, like the good little cook she was, the three others thought they would enjoy themselves going on 'a tour of the property', as George proudly put it.

Nothing seemed to have changed since last year. There were a few broken branches lying about, which showed that there had been some high winds during the winter, but the castle walls hadn't lost any more of their stones.

'Come on, lunch-time!' said Dick, as the three cousins made their way back to their camp. 'Gosh, I'm ravenous!'

'Woof!' said Timmy, wagging his tail to show he agreed.

'I'm hungry as a hunter myself,' said Julian.

But George was lagging behind, looking out at the horizon. She loved the sea – it meant adventure to her!

'I wonder,' she murmured to herself, 'yes, I wonder if we'll come across some sort of mystery to do with the sea this time …?'

'George, that's just wishful thinking,' Dick

teased her. 'You'd love to see a nice juicy mystery washed up for you by the sea, wouldn't you? Honestly, what an imagination you've got!'

But George wasn't going to rise to his teasing. Still gazing out to sea, she insisted, 'You can laugh at me if you like, Dick – all right, I know I *do* have some wild ideas – but all the same, I've got a funny feeling that there *is* an adventure waiting for us here! Right at our feet!'

*Chapter Two*

## A FIERCE STORM

The children spent the next five days happily camping on Kirrin Island. The weather stayed fine, and George, her cousins and Timmy were having a really lovely time.

As soon as they woke up in the morning they had a big breakfast, with plenty of eggs and bacon and fried bread. Then they went off to bathe and swim, or look for shells on the beach, or they ran races and played ball in the water. They could talk and talk at meal-times and make all the noise they liked! In the afternoons they went out in the rowing boat, or went bathing again, or just lay in the sun. When evening came they lit their camp fire, Dick and George played their mouth organs, and Anne sang songs in her sweet little voice. Julian sometimes accompanied his sister on his guitar, and if the others wanted a story he always knew a good one to tell.

But that wasn't all the fun they had! There were long games of hide and seek, card games, guessing games, trials of skill, all sorts of activities. When their provisions ran low the Five got into George's rowing boat and went over to Kirrin Cottage to stock up – or else they went to Kirrin village, either by road on their fine new bicycles that Uncle Quentin had given them, or rowing round by sea in the boat.

They all liked wandering round the village on market day, looking at the stalls in the market place. Altogether, the Five were having a wonderful holiday.

And then, on the sixth day, something happened!

'I say!' Julian exclaimed that morning when he emerged from the tent he was sharing with Dick. 'I say, just look at that sky! The weather's going to change, if you ask me!'

George, who was just coming back from washing her face at the spring, agreed with him.

'Yes, it is,' she said. 'See those big black clouds in the west? And the rising sun is red as a lobster!'

'Red sky in the morning, shepherd's warning,' said Dick wisely.

'You're right,' said George. 'And the wind's getting up too. I wouldn't be surprised if we had a good storm before evening.'

Anne groaned. 'Storms are *never* "good"!' she

protested. '*I* think we ought to pack up and go back to the cottage straight away, George. Remember, Aunt Fanny and Uncle Quentin made us promise to go home if the weather turned bad.'

'Oh, they just said that because they felt they ought to!' said George, who didn't want to leave her island. 'Anyway, at the moment it's still fine and the sun's shining, so let's wait till it rains and turns cold before we think about going back. After all, it's not very far from here to the mainland, is it, Timmy?' she added, turning to her dog.

'Woof!' replied Timmy, wagging his tail.

In fact, George would far rather have been marooned on her island by a storm than shut up in Kirrin Cottage, where they couldn't play any noisy games in case they disturbed her father's work! Uncle Quentin was a famous scientist. George loved and admired him – but she did sometimes think it was rather a nuisance having somebody like that as a father!

'George is right,' said Dick cheerfully. 'Let's make the most of the fine weather while it's still here! Who's for an underwater swimming race? The winner gets the best of the shells we've found!'

George thought that was a fine idea, Julian let himself be tempted by it too, and so Anne had to do as the others did.

And that was how it all began, because if the children *had* decided to go back to the mainland that day they would never have had the exciting adventure the storm wind was blowing their way!

Late in the morning, when the children had swum enough races at last, they realised that the sun was just disappearing behind a wall of big black clouds. Almost at once, the sky seemed to open and torrents of rain came pouring down on the island and the Five.

George, Julian, Dick, Anne and Timmy ran back to their camp as fast as their legs would carry them – or in Timmy's case his paws.

'Quick!' cried George. 'Take the tents down and carry everything into the castle. At least we'll be under cover there inside the room which still has a roof on it!'

'Oh, bother!' said Julian crossly, pulling a tent peg. 'It's my fault – I should have insisted on going back. And now it's too late!'

'You're right there, old boy,' said Dick, pointing to the coast of the mainland. 'Look at that! You can't even see land.'

The rain was falling even faster now, and the wind was howling, threatening to blow away the little tent with the provisions in it. Anne quickly stuffed them into a big bag. The three others were hard at work folding the wet canvas of the tents. It was whipping round their legs.

'Thank goodness we're in our bathing things!' gasped Julian. 'This is just like having a showerbath! I wouldn't put a dog out in this – would *you*, Timmy?'

Timmy, who hated rain, was already running to the castle for shelter, barking as loud as he could to invite George to hurry up and follow him! At last, all of the Five were inside the shelter of the castle's thick walls.

'I say, that wind was icy!' said Dick. 'I'm freezing! Why don't we light a fire?'

'Good idea!' agreed George. 'What luck we've got a stack of dry firewood in here!'

The children dried themselves thoroughly and got thick woolly pullovers out of their duffle bags. Once they were nice and warm, with the fire burning cheerfully and a good hot meal of sausages and beans in tomato sauce cooked by Anne inside them, they had nothing to do but sit and enjoy watching the storm.

It was one of the fiercest storms they had ever seen. If they went to stand just inside the ruined arch of the castle doorway on the side of the island which fell sheer to the sea, they could watch the sea as well as the sky. The sight was fascinating. Thunder was rolling round the dark sky, and the sea looked dark too, and dangerous. Huge waves came crashing against the cliff as if they wanted to swallow up the island, the castle, and the Five standing there above the foaming sea.

It was one of the fiercest storms they had ever seen.

'Oh, isn't it frightening?' quavered Anne, who didn't like it much. 'All that rough water, and the lightning flashes!'

'Close your eyes if you're scared!' said George, rather impatiently. 'You know perfectly well you're not in any danger here, Anne!'

'We can't possibly take the boat out in this,' said Julian gloomily. 'We'd be sure to be shipwrecked! What a good thing I pulled the boat right up on the beach! I just hope it doesn't blow away.'

'It's in a sheltered place,' said George. 'And luckily I thought of putting a tarpaulin over it this morning, so we're sure to find it safe and sound again.'

'But Aunt Fanny and Uncle Quentin will be so worried!' said Anne, sounding worried herself.

'No, they won't,' said George. 'They'll know we had enough sense to stay under cover here in the castle, so for goodness' sake don't fuss!'

Meanwhile, the storm was getting worse and worse the whole time. When evening came it was still raging, and even in the middle of the night the children could hear the wind howling fiercely and the sea growling like some angry wild beast. Lying on a piece of canvas spread on the floor of the room and nice and warm in their sleeping bags, they felt very glad they had thick walls all round to protect them – and a roof which was absolutely waterproof, thanks to the work Uncle Quentin had had done on the castle to make sure it was safe.

Suddenly a tremendous noise made them all jump! The sea was battering the cliff again, and the sound of waves breaking was followed by such a crash you would have thought the castle itself was falling down. George, Julian, Dick and Anne struggled out of their sleeping bags and got to their feet. Timmy barked in protest. And outside the noise still went on, but now it had turned into a whole series of strange crashing sounds one after the other.

'Whatever's going on?' whispered Anne. She was very pale, and she drew closer to her big brother as if she hoped he would protect her against any unknown dangers. 'It sounds as if the castle's collapsing!'

'No, no!' Julian told her. 'We're all right here! You can see the walls are standing perfectly firm all around us.'

'It's something outside!' said George, making for the arched doorway above the cliff top.

Dick followed his cousin, and the two of them marched boldly out into the rain, straining their eyes to see all they could. Soon they realised that part of the cliff down below had been under-mined by the violent waves and bits of it were falling into the sea – they were making the queer noises the children had heard. The wind battered the cliff so hard that George felt the ground was moving!

'An earthquake!' she cried. 'That really puts the lid on it!'

Of course it wasn't really an earthquake, but it felt like it, with the sea so rough and the cliff crumbling away down below!

'What luck your father had those supports put in to prop up the castle ruins!' said Dick. 'I'd say those old stones of yours are standing steadier than the rocks down there at the foot of the cliff. Gosh, look at those waves! What a sight!'

It was certainly a magnificent, awe-inspiring spectacle. The huge waves came rolling in and breaking one after another. Suddenlt, one like a miniature tidal wave crashed against the cliff! The water shot up to an amazing height, spraying in the air. Then, almost at once, things went back to normal. The waves calmed down, the wind dropped, and the storm was over!

However, once they were back in their sleeping bags the four children, and even Timmy, had difficulty getting to sleep. They lay listening to the last echoes of the storm dying down, and when they finally did drop off it was almost dawn.

When they woke up next morning the previous day's storm was only a memory. Anne was the first out of the castle. She gave a cry of delight, and told the others 'Oh, the sky's all blue and fresh as if it had just been washed, and the sun's shining again!'

'Let's take the rowing boat and go tell your parents we're all right, George,' suggested Julian. 'Then we'll stock up with provisions and –'

'And come back here to put the tents up again!' George finished. 'Yes, all right, but first we must go round the island to see how much damage the storm has done.'

It didn't take the children long to make their tour of inspection. They found two trees completely uprooted, and several others with broken branches, but altogether the island had stood up to the storm better than they'd expected . It was the cliff that seemed to have suffered most.

Standing there on the cliff top, George craned her neck to get a better view of the rocks below.

'Careful!' said Julian. 'Don't go so close to the edge, George! It's dangerous, specially after last night's rock-falls.'

'Ju, I think I can see something! There – down below!'

'Where?' asked Dick, interested, craning over to see for himself.

A few pebbles rolled away from under his feet, and Julian firmly held his brother back and then pulled George away from the edge too.

'That'll do!' he said firmly. 'I don't want you

two ending up in pieces on the rocks down there!'

'Oh, Julian!' said George excitedly. 'I really *did* see something, you know – something really extraordinary!'

'What was it?'

'A long black shape on the sea-bed! It wasn't moving, and it was quite close to that big rock – you know the one I mean, where the water's calm and very deep!'

'We *don't* know what you mean!' Dick interrupted. He sounded disbelieving. 'The water *is* deep there – so you couldn't possibly have seen anything on the bottom!'

'That's just the point!' said George. 'That's what surprises me, too! The black shape I saw looked like a sunken ship. A bit of an underwater wreck!'

## Chapter Three

## THE GOLDEN GALLEON

'Oh, come on, George, old thing! Your imagination's running away with you again!' said Julian, with a smile.

'No, it isn't!' George protested. 'I'm *sure* I saw it – I saw the skeleton of a ship! Or maybe it was a dead whale.'

'A dead whale would float,' Julian pointed out.

'Well then, it must be a ship!'

'But how could you see it if the water's so deep there?' Dick insisted.

George thought for a moment.

'It's true that the water *was* deep there,' she said at last. 'But that was *before* the storm! I know just what the sea is like round my island – but all those tremendous waves yesterday, and that bit of cliff falling in, may have changed the shape of the sea bottom. Suppose a lot of silt and stones were washed up among the rocks in the deep water ...'

The other children's eyes began to shine.

'Yes,' said Julian, 'you may be right, George. The stormy sea could have jolted the wreck free of the silt that was holding it down, too.'

'We just have to find out if you really *did* see what you thought you saw!' Dick added.

George scowled. 'If you don't believe me, just go and look!' she said huffily. Then she smiled again. 'Yes, that's an idea! Let's take the boat and tow out to the big flat rock. Once we're out there we should be able to see it quite easily!'

The boys were already making for the steep path leading down to the cove. George soon caught up, and Anne, with her fair hair floating in the gentle breeze, hurried after them. Timmy, who was pleased to get a chance of a good run, was leaping round his mistress and barking. You might have thought he *knew* there was an adventure on the horizon!

Just as George and Julian had hoped, the rowing boat, carefully pulled well up on to the beach and covered with a tarpaulin, had not suffered at all from the rough waves and wind. The children hauled it down the beach again and pushed it into the water. Then they clambered in, Timmy included. Once they were all settled, Dick and George each took a pair of oars.

They rowed round the island. All four cousins felt rather excited as they came close to the flat rock. They were soon at the foot of the tall cliff, and they could see where part of it had crumbled away last night. The flat rock itself was some way out, but the boat wasn't long in reaching it. George and Dick stopped rowing and leaned overboard to look down into the depths of the sea.

But unfortunately, all the little waves slapping round the big rock meant they didn't get a very good view.

'Oh, bother! I could see better from right up above!' said George, disappointed.

'I thought this might happen,' said Julian. 'So I brought along one of our inflatable mattresses – the one with the transparent peephole in it.'

'Oh, good!' cried George. 'Quick, hand it over!'

In a trice they had the mattress blown up and floating on the water, safely secured by a rope to the boat a little way from the rock. George lay flat on top of it, looked down through the peephole and gave a cry of delight.

'A wreck! Yes, it *is* a wreck!'

She had been right! There below her lay the hull of a boat, proving she hadn't been imagining things.

Eager to see it too, Dick, Anne and Julian took turns on the mattress and looked down below the surface of the water. Sure enough, George *had* been right! They could all see the shape of a boat lying on its side under the water.

'But how odd!' said Julian. 'Did you others notice what that boat looks like?'

'Like nothing I've ever seen before!' said George. 'Except in a rather bad film when I went to the cinema once!'

'*I* know what it looks like,' said Dick. 'A modern yacht disguised to look like one of those Spanish ships of the old days – what did they call them? Caravels or something!'

'That's right!' agreed Anne, remembering one of the illustrations in a picture dictionary she had at home. 'It was a kind of galleon the Spanish sailors used to carry gold.'

'My word!' murmured Julian. 'If we hadn't all seen the same thing I'd think *I* was imagining things for a change, not George!'

George ran her fingers through her hair. She was really excited by their discovery, and her eyes were shining. She told herself that the funny feeling she had had was quite right. The Five *were* going to have an adventure! Here it was, at their very feet – although some way below the surface of the water, of course!

'Listen!' cried George. 'Do you know what we're going to do?'

'Explore this wreck straight away, of course!' said Dick.

'Right! You and Anne have frogman masks,

and Julian and I have those diving outfits of ours with oxygen flasks. If ever there was a good time to use them it's now! What luck we keep them in the boat!'

As she spoke, George was opening a little locker in the bows of her rowing boat. She got out the diving things and handed them round. Quickly, she put on her flippers and the harness to hold the oxygen flask on her back. Anne helped her adjust the straps. Julian was getting ready too, with Dick helping him.

Dick and Anne were just about to put their own diving masks on when George and Julian both moved to stop them. 'Hang on!' said George. 'We don't all want to go down at once. And now I think of it, I'd say that wreck is too deep for anyone to go down without extra oxygen, anyway.'

'That's what I think too,' Julian agreed. 'And I don't want Anne going down at all. She's too young. Dick, you can borrow my equipment and go down when I come up, if you like.'

If Anne was disappointed she didn't show it. She was a sensible, sweet-natured little girl who didn't mind obeying her elder brother, and all she did was heave a little sigh.

George, who was impatient to go down, was the first to dive in. Julian went into the water just a moment after her. They had agreed for a start they would only swim around the wreck

George and Julian stared in amazement. They were gold bars — ingots, all yellow and shiny!

and look at it from the outside.

Up above them, Dick, Anne and Timmy were trying to follow their movements. The cousins swam slowly down, and soon reached the wreck. It didn't seem quite so impressive close to, but all the same it did look very queer. George and Julian were puzzled.

'No doubt about it,' thought George, 'it certainly *is* a modern yacht!'

And Julian was thinking along the same lines. 'This boat can't have sunk very long ago. The brass and chrome fittings are tarnished, of course, and the hull's covered with shells and seaweed – but there doesn't seem to be much oxydisation, and that layer of barnacles and weed isn't a very thick one. How odd!'

What surprised the two cousins most was the fact that in spite of its basic shape and its modern fittings, in some ways the strange boat *did* remind them of those old Spanish galleons. It had a very tall forecastle with elaborate decorations on it, and the hull itself had a rail round it covered with moulding and curlicues which were quite out of place on a modern yacht. The wreck really was a most extraordinary-looking vessel. They couldn't make it out.

Swimming round to a brass plate which was half hidden under strings of seaweed, George cleared the weed away, with some difficulty, and the name of the mysterious yacht came into view.

Julian joined his cousin and read the words over her shoulder. The boat was called *The Golden Galleon*.

George turned round and pointed to the surface of the water above them. With a few movements of their flippers, she and Julian went up to rejoin Dick, Anne and Timmy.

'Well?' asked Dick impatiently.

'Well,' said George, taking her mask off, 'the wreck itself is quite a puzzle! And we don't even know what it may contain yet. But the outside –'

'What *about* the outside?' asked Dick, as she hesitated.

Julian took over from George and described what they had seen. *The Golden Galleon* was a kind of freak ship built in two different styles! The children longed to know why it looked so odd.

'Now we must find out what's inside the yacht!' said George, putting her mask on again. 'I'm going back down! Coming, Dick?'

Dick borrowed his brother's equipment, as they had agreed – although Julian wasn't too happy about it. During his rapid exploration he had noticed that although the wreck was lying on a shoal it was right on the edge of what seemed to be some very deep water. He wondered if they could be sure there wasn't any danger of it slipping off the shoal.

'Look here, I don't think you two ought to go

inside the wreck on your own,' he said. 'Promise me that all you'll do on this trip is have a look at the deck. Then I'll go down again myself!'

Reluctantly, George and Dick agreed. George dived into the water, and Dick followed her. This time George let herself drop neatly on to the deck of the ship, which stood at a sloping angle, and Dick joined her there. Holding the handrail, the young explorers went cautiously forward. The planks beneath their feet turned out to be all slippery and slimy. It wasn't nice touching them, and the two cousins made faces of disgust. Shoals of little fishes swam away ahead of them.

Soon George and Dick came to an open hatchway with a dark space beyond it. Quite forgetting that she had promised Julian not to go inside the wreck, George started to swim in. Dick was going to remind her that she shouldn't, but of course he could not make her hear him. So he hurried after her to try and tell her in sign language to be careful.

But oh dear! Just as Dick was putting his hand on George's shoulder, the wreck moved beneath their feet. The yacht shifted off balance and began slipping towards the deep water.

The sudden movement threw Dick and George against one another. They clung to the bulkhead near them as hard as they could. George quickly grasped what they must do.

Grabbing Dick's wrist, she pulled him through the opening again.

Once out of the wreck, the two of them kicked out hard so as to swim upwards and clear of the deck. They felt they had nearly had a very nasty accident, and they hurried up to the surface as fast as they could go, escaping from the eddying current which seemed likely to pull the ship over into the deep water.

'Julian! Anne!' cried George, removing her mask as soon as she hauled herself up on the big flat rock beside the rowing boat. 'Oh, what awful bad luck! We shan't be able to explore *The Golden Galleon* any more! We'll never know its secret now! It's sinking back into deep water.'

Dick, who wasn't quite so worked up, looked down into the depths of the sea below them.

'You're letting your imagination work overtime as usual, old thing!' he told her. 'Yes, the wreck certainly shifted – but it didn't sink any deeper. It's still there – and it looks as if it'll stay put now!'

'*Looks* as if it'll stay put? How do you know?' asked Julian, worried. 'I never ought to have let you two go down! Give me my diving kit, Dick. I'm going down again – I want to see for myself.'

'I'll come with you!' said George. She had cheered up as soon as she saw that their wreck was still there after all.

'Do be careful!' begged Anne, who thought it was rather frightening.

'Woof! Woof!' barked Timmy disapprovingly. The intelligent dog hated seeing George disappear into the water. He couldn't follow her where she was going – and that meant he couldn't protect her.

Cautiously, the two divers went down. Julian had insisted on going first, and though George was usually the leader in the children's adventures, she gave way to him. She knew that Uncle Quentin expected Julian, as the eldest, to look after the safety of the other three.

When Julian reached the wreck, he was pleased and relieved to see that though it had certainly slipped, it hadn't moved towards the deeper water, but in the other direction. Now it was lodged firmly between some rocks which were holding it almost upright. Exploring it would be easier now it was in this new position.

Julian gestured cheerfully to his cousin, making a thumbs-up sign. But George didn't need that to understand what he meant! Her heart was thumping! Now she could get inside the wrecked yacht and explore its mysterious depths.

His fears calmed, Julian was examining the deck of the sunken yacht with interest. George slipped inside. At first she couldn't see much. Then a faint light from above showed her a long gangway at the bottom of a ladder. She went down.

George had taken the precaution of bringing a

waterproof torch with her and, as there wasn't enough light to see by once she was down the ladder, she switched it on. Some fascinating discoveries lay ahead of her! *The Golden Galleon* turned out to be a splendid modern yacht, most luxuriously fitted-out. George admired the elegant saloon, the comfortable cabins, the kitchen – but there was one door which wouldn't open. What could the cabin behind it hold?

She pushed in vain. The door wouldn't budge. She thought it was locked, and not just jammed.

'I must tell Julian,' George said to herself.

She was going to go back on deck and look for her cousin, but as she was passing the saloon she saw him there, glancing at the gramophone records. She signalled to him to follow her.

When they reached the door that wouldn't open they both struggled with the lock. Eventually Julian took out the knife he had hitched to the belt of his diving outfit, and put the point of it into the keyhole. He turned it to right and to left and, much to his surprise, the lock gave way. He hadn't expected to succeed so quickly!

George was already pushing him in, eager to get inside herself. The two cousins found themselves in a cabin which was larger than the others. Maybe it had belonged to the captain of the vessel! Three heavy wooden crates stood in a corner, piled one on top of the other. Julian went

Anne helped George adjust her straps. Julian was getting ready too.

The wreck was really a most extraordinary-looking vessel.

over to them. The lids were nailed down, but sea-water had rotted the planks in places. The best way Julian could think of to open them was by giving them a few kicks!

Once again he succeeded better than he could have hoped for. The bottom crate suddenly gave way, and the other two, with nothing to hold them up any longer, collapsed as well. Their contents spilled out on the floor.

George and Julian stared in amazement, eyes popping as they gazed at the objects at their feet.

They were gold bars – ingots, all yellow and shiny, and hardly tarnished at all by the time they had spent lying at the bottom of the sea!

## Chapter Four

## AN ALARMING INCIDENT!

Recovering from their surprise, George and Julian exchanged meaningful looks. Where did the gold come from? Whose was it? Why was it on board the shipwrecked yacht? There were so many questions, and they didn't know the answers to any of them!

George bent down to pick up one of the ingots. It was a queer feeling to be holding something which must be worth so much money. She turned to Julian, still holding the gold ingot, and signed to him that she thought it would be a good idea to go back to the surface. She was thinking that they ought to discuss their find with Dick and Anne. Julian nodded in reply.

So the two cousins left the cabin containing the treasure and went back into the gangway.

41

George was still clutching the gold ingot. She was in front of Julian, and was making for the ladder which led up to the deck when suddenly an undulating shadow passed in front of her. In the dim light from above, George saw that it was a big, long fish.

'It could be a conger eel or something like that!' she told herself, shuddering slightly.

She didn't like the idea of a slimy, snaky eel touching her, so she thought she would frighten it away. Switching on her waterproof torch, she turned its beam on the creature. But far from being scared off, the eel or whatever it was seemed annoyed by the bright light – it made straight for George! And George was horrified to see that it wasn't a conger eel at all. It was a shark!

Of course it was not a man-eating shark, only a dogfish shark, the kind that finds its way into European waters. All the same, it *was* a shark – and an angry one too!

Half blinded by the torch, the big fish was making for the source of the light that dazzled it, as if it wanted to destroy the torch. It nearly knocked George over, even though she had flinched away.

Julian had seen the fish too, and he realised they were in danger. Dogfish sharks are usually very timid and will swim away if they meet divers, but this one, as they could see, was an exception. It turned abruptly and made for George again, with its little mouth full of pointed teeth already open, ready to bite.

George had the presence of mind to drop her torch, which went out. But now she couldn't see, so she didn't know where the fish was coming from. At that moment Julian grabbed her ankle, pulled it, and sent her falling over backwards. Just in time! The dogfish shark shot on above them, carried on its way by its own impetus. But suppose it came back?

George and Julian both turned towards the ladder leading up on deck. However, they hadn't reached it when the fish came swimming along the gangway in their direction again. It was a nasty moment.

This time George decided she really *would* scare the fish away properly, and she began agitating the water with her arms and her flippers. Guessing what his cousin's idea was, Julian copied her. The unexpected noise and the unusual eddies in the water surprised the shark. It swerved aside, and after hesitating for a moment or so – it seemed a terribly long time to the children! – it darted off over their heads and disappeared.

George and Julian would have to go the same way as the fish if they wanted to leave the wreck.

'I just hope it's not up there waiting for us!' thought Julian.

But George, who knew more than he did about the sea and its creatures, knew that a frightened fish is quick to swim away from danger, and hardly ever comes back to confront it. So she was not at all scared as she kicked out and came up to the deck again.

A couple of minutes later, she and Julian were back in safety with Dick and Anne.

Seeing his little mistress come up above the water, Timmy jumped for joy and nearly fell overboard. George took off her mask, and the dog washed her face lovingly with his tongue.

'My goodness, you do look pale, George!' cried Anne, in concern. 'Are you very cold?'

'No, just tired,' said George. 'Three dives in a row –'

'And rather a lot of excitement!' Julian finished for her. 'We discovered a treasure and nearly got eaten by a shark!'

Dick laughed. He thought his brother was joking, and he decided to join in the fun.

'Yes,' he said, 'and while you were down there Anne and I discovered a shark and nearly ate a treasure!'

'Don't be such an idiot!' sighed George wearily. She really *was* tired! 'Julian's only telling the exact truth. I was actually bringing back a gold ingot to show you when that horrible fish attacked me. I had to let go of the ingot to defend myself – and then, in all the confusion, I went and lost my torch too!' She grinned at Julian. 'Thanks, Ju! But for you, I bet that shark would have had me for lunch!'

Dick stopped laughing. Anne gave a little cry of surprise and alarm. Just as if he understood what they were saying, Timmy jumped on the flat rock and planted himself there, paws apart and head on one side. You would have thought he knew he was going to hear the details of an exciting story!

When George had finished telling the others about her adventure, Anne cried, 'Oh, we must go straight back to Kirrin Cottage to tell Uncle Quentin about it! I'm sure he'll know what to do!'

'Yes,' said Julian. 'He'll know who to tell so that we can find out who owns that gold.'

George was quite ready for action again. She was rather cross that she had had to abandon the gold ingot she was bringing up, but she did hope this wasn't the end of the adventure for herself and her cousins.

'If it hadn't been for that nasty shark I could have brought back proof of what we saw,' she was thinking as they rowed towards the mainland.

Once back on shore, the four cousins moored the boat and ran to Kirrin Cottage. Aunt Fanny heaved a sigh of relief at the sight of them.

'Hallo, children! Oh, I'm so glad to see you! I

was really worried about you in that dreadful storm! Now, off you go to the kitchen, and make yourselves some nice hot cocoa. There's a sponge cake just out of the oven, too.'

But though George loved cocoa and her mother's sponge cakes, she decided their news must come first.

'Where's Father?' she asked. 'We've got to tell him something at once – and you too!'

'Your father's very busy today, George dear. He's shut himself up in his study, and he says he doesn't want to be disturbed all day. And there's some shopping I really *must* get done in the village. I'm sure your story can wait! See you this evening!'

Disappointed, George, Julian, Dick and Anne watched Aunt Fanny go off to the village. They would just have to wait patiently! However, the delicious sponge with raspberry jam filling was some consolation.

Uncle Quentin had been so wrapped up in his work that he was late for supper that evening. When he did come in, the children immediately began telling him and Aunt Fanny about their strange adventure. Uncle Quentin looked very interested.

'Why, this is fascinating!' he cried. '*The Golden Galleon*, you said? The name reminds me of something – now what was it? Oh yes, I remember! It's the name of the yacht which

46

was in the news so much two years or so ago.'

'Yes, I remember now, too,' said Aunt Fanny. 'It was a very odd boat, specially built for an American who was odder still! His name was Mr Wilson, and he wanted a yacht with all modern conveniences, but looking as much like an old Spanish galleon as possible!' She laughed, and added, 'In fact, I remember seeing it shown on the television news. It was perfectly ridiculous – a freak of a boat!'

'Aunt Fanny, was Mr Wilson a gold bullion dealer?' Anne asked straight out.

Aunt Fanny laughed again. 'A gold bullion dealer? Good gracious, no! Anything like that is done by the Bank of England, you know, not private people. And if you're thinking Mr Wilson might have been smuggling the gold on his boat, he wouldn't have needed to do anything like that – he was a millionaire anyway!'

'But where do those gold ingots come from, then?' asked Julian.

'Wait a minute, my boy!' said his uncle, thinking hard. 'If I remember correctly, the yacht was stolen while it was anchored near Kirrin! Mr Wilson had come to this part of the country for a holiday – he did that every year. And he was on shore with his guests at the time.'

Dick looked very surprised.

'Goodness me – who would have wanted to

steal a yacht like that?' he cried. 'I mean, it would have been recognised straight away!'

'Yes, of course. But the thing is that it was a very fast boat – and the gangsters who took it wanted to get away from the country as fast as they possibly could!'

'Why?' asked George.

'Because they'd just robbed a bank!' explained Uncle Quentin. 'They took the gold ingots on board and went off in *The Golden Galleon*. It certainly lived up to its name that particular day!'

'And I can guess the rest!' said George. 'The yacht sank – perhaps because the bank robbers didn't know how to handle it? So it went down with them and the gold on board!'

'That's almost what happened, but not quite,' her father told her. 'The yacht was lost in a storm very much like the one we had yesterday. But the gangsters escaped in the lifeboat – they were rescued from the sea and then sent to prison. There were three of them. Now what were they called? Yes, I remember, their names were Bates, Farley and Sanderson. They always denied stealing the gold ingots – all they would admit to was taking the yacht, and they insisted that they had only borrowed that "for fun". In fact, that was all that could actually be proved against them, so they didn't get very long prison sentences. Once they've served them they'll be released.'

'They have just been released,' interrupted Aunt Fanny. 'I read it in the paper only the other day!'

'But I don't see why no one tried to salvage the yacht and the treasure on board,' said George.

'Well, people did try to,' replied Uncle Quentin. 'But the gangsters had been very vague about exactly *where* the yacht was wrecked – as we can see now! You found *The Golden Galleon* quite close to land, whereas it was thought to have been lost well out to sea, quite a long way from here!'

George jumped to her feet.

'If the bank robbers didn't say where they were shipwrecked, that was probably on purpose!' she cried. 'First, because the discovery of the gold would have given them away, and second, because they had probably planned to go back and get it for themselves once they were out of prison!'

'Yes, that's what I think too,' Uncle Quentin told her. 'So it's very important to let the authorities know as soon as possible. I'll start by telephoning the police station. The police will know what to do.'

It was getting quite late, but the rather sleepy voice which answered Uncle Quentin's telephone call suddenly became *very* wide awake when the policeman heard the exciting news! After a short conversation, Uncle Quentin hung up, smiling.

'They're clearing the decks for action!' he said. 'But I don't suppose they'll be able to do anything much until tomorrow. Well, children, it's bedtime. Sleep well! And congratulations on your remarkable discovery!'

## Chapter Five

## WHERE ARE THE INGOTS?

George slept badly that night. She dreamed about treasures, bank robbers – and sharks! She was up at dawn, pestering her cousins to get up too.

'Come on! Oh, do hurry and get ready! I'm sure they'll be needing us to show them where the wreck is!'

But it wasn't until nearly three in the afternoon that a party of policemen arrived. There was an inspector with them, and two frogmen. The inspector took down statements from Julian and George, and then asked the children to accompany him to the scene of the wreck. Julian and Dick pushed George's rowing boat out into the water, and the coastguards' launch, which had come along to help the police, took it in tow. The children were on top of the world!

George would have liked to dive with the frogmen. The shark and any of its friends would have gone off, alarmed by the sound of an engine and all the disturbance, so there would be nothing more to fear from them! But Inspector Bond wouldn't hear of it. Julian steered the rowing boat over to the flat rock, and once they were there the Five had to content themselves with watching. They didn't like that at all!

They saw the two frogmen leave the launch and disappear below the surface. After a little while – though it seemed ages and ages to George – the two men came up again.

'They've come up for the metal containers the police brought to hold the gold ingots,' Dick said confidently.

But he was wrong. Inspector Bond, who was sitting in the launch, turned to the Five and shouted, 'Well, kids, you must have been dreaming! There aren't any gold bars down there! You weren't making it all up, were you? If so, you'd better come clean now!'

For a moment the four children were taken aback.

'You mean you haven't found *The Golden Galleon*?' George finally asked, when she had her voice back.

'Oh yes! The wreck's just where you said we'd find it, but though our frogmen saw some loose planks floating about which *could* have come from those crates you mentioned, there wasn't any sign of gold ingots!'

This time the children exchanged glances of consternation. And then everyone went over to Kirrin Island to try and work it out. Julian and George swore their statements about the gold ingots were true. As for the frogmen, *they* assured the Inspector they hadn't found anything – not even the one gold bar George had dropped in the gangway. It was only too obvious what had happened! The bank robbers, who had served their sentences and just been let out of prison, had moved too fast for the police and had got their loot back!

A little later the policemen left the island in the coastguards' launch, leaving George and her cousins both puzzled and disappointed.

'They're going to make inquiries,' sighed Julian, 'but will anything come of that? The bank robbers must be well away by now!'

'I'm not so sure of that,' said George. 'The gold ingots were still there in the wreck yesterday, so they were removed quite recently. And they must be very heavy to carry!'

'That wouldn't matter if the gangsters have a van or car of some sort,' Dick pointed out.

'The Inspector radioed back to land, telling his men to set up road blocks on all the main roads in this part of the country,' Anne reminded them in her soft voice.

'It may have been too late,' said Julian. 'Oh, well, there's nothing more we can do, so let's forget about it! The sun's shining – why don't we make the most of being here on Kirrin Island in fine weather again?'

After the delicious picnic tea Aunt Fanny had prepared for them, Dick switched on his little pocket radio to listen to the news, and by a coincidence the newsreader was just mentioning the disappearance of the gold ingots.

'No suspicious vehicle has attempted to pass the police checkpoints on the main roads,' the announcer was saying. 'It is possible that the bank robbers got away from the area before the roadblocks were set up, but this is not very probable, because speedy but thorough police inquiries have established that no unfamiliar vehicle was seen in the Kirrin area either yesterday, last night or today.'

George jumped up in excitement.

'You see? My guess was right! The gangsters *have* got the gold ingots back, but they haven't got them away from here yet. They thought there wasn't any hurry! They couldn't know that we'd discovered their loot and told the police. They may be somewhere quite close with the gold – and kicking themselves for not having taken it away earlier!'

'Do you really think the bank robbers may be somewhere close?' asked Julian.

George leaned back against a rock and faced her cousins, folding her arms.

'I'm sure they are!' she replied. 'Bates, Farley and Sanderson must have gone to ground somewhere near Kirrin. And now they're waiting for the police to stop keeping such a close watch on the roads – then they'll think they can make off with the gold. But we won't let them! This is a job for the Five – we must find those bank robbers and get them arrested!'

Julian, Dick and Anne thought that was a very good idea. Timmy seemed to agree too. But the days passed by and neither the police nor the Five seemed to be getting any nearer to finding the three men! The children spent most of their time riding round the countryside on their new bicycles, on the alert for anything odd, but nothing turned up! They didn't find so much as the sniff of a trail. They would go back to Kirrin in the afternoons, tired and disappointed at having to admit they were getting nowhere, and then they went back to their camp on the island for the night.

One evening the Five were sitting round their camp fire after supper. It was a warm night. Anne looked up at the sky. 'The stars look just like diamonds glittering on a piece of black velvet,' she sighed. 'I suppose that sounds a bit silly, but it's true, isn't it?'

'Woof!' barked Timmy. He was taking a great

Inside, George was quietly fuming with annoyance.

A grunt from Timmy woke George — she was wide awake at once.

interest in a hedgehog going for its evening walk.

Dick was playing his mouth organ softly, and Julian strummed on his guitar. George was the only one who didn't seem in tune with the peace of the evening. Inside, she was quietly fuming with annoyance.

'This is the first time we've ever spent so long trying to solve a mystery without getting any results at all!' she suddenly burst out. 'But I'm not giving up! Tomorrow we'll start again, combing the whole countryside, being extra careful not to miss anything! We must ask people questions – someone may have noticed strangers about at the time we're interested in. And we must search any place that looks as if it could possibly be a hiding place for the treasure – because the gangsters may have just hidden the gold ingots somewhere, meaning to come back and fetch them later!'

The four cousins discussed it all for quite a long time before they went to their two tents for the night. Timmy lay down beside his mistress, as he did every evening, and soon the campers fell asleep.

It must have been past midnight when a grunt from Timmy woke George. She was wide awake at once, and she put her hand on the dog's head to make him be quiet.

'Ssh!' she said, listening. She could hear

masculine voices. 'Julian and Dick,' she thought at first. But no, that wasn't her cousins talking! Very cautiously, she got up and went out of the tent, with Timmy following her.

Outside she stopped dead in surprise. Two men had just climbed the steep path from the beach, with nothing but the bright moonlight to show the way. Pebbles crunched under their feet. They were certainly making themselves at home here! Acting on impulse as usual, George did not hesitate for a moment. 'Hey! You!' she shouted. 'You're not allowed to land here, you know! This island is private property!'

In her pyjamas, she looked so like a boy that the newcomers thought she *was* one!

One of the men uttered an exclamation. 'You heard what that lad said, Harry? There are people on the island! If I'd known . . .!'

'Yes – this upsets our plans, doesn't it?' muttered his companion under his breath.

Roused by the noise, Dick and Julian, followed by Anne, came out of the tents too. The man who had spoken first pointed.

'Look, it's nothing but a bunch of kids camping out! They don't matter!'

And the two strangers were calmly walking on without taking the slightest notice of what George had said! She was infuriated by their insolence.

'I order you to leave at once!' she said. 'Or I'll set my dog on you!'

The two men – she could see now that they looked very rough – exchanged glances and then burst into laughter.

'Did you ever hear anything like it?' said the first man. 'Just listen to that young pipsqueak laying down the law! We'll soon make *him* pipe down!'

It was Julian's turn to step in.

'This is my cousin Georgina's island,' he said, pointing to George. 'It's her own personal property, and you're trespassing!'

What happened next happened so fast that later the children remembered it only as a kind of nightmare!

The man called Harry just pushed Julian aside with the back of his hand. Then he grabbed George by the wrist.

So you're a girl, are you? Well, listen to me, little girl! I'm giving the orders, understand? You'll keep quiet, or else!'

George didn't need to call Timmy to her aid. In one bound, the intelligent animal was on the gangster, sinking his teeth into the man's upper arm. Harry howled, but he managed to force Timmy's jaws open and make him let go – and then, seizing the dog's collar, he tied it very tightly to the trunk of a nearby tree. Hardly able to move and half strangled, poor Timmy couldn't even bark.

'You great brute!' cried George, flinging herself at Harry.

But the other man caught hold of her. Taking another piece of cord from his pocket, he tied *her* to the tree too, just above Timmy. At the same time Harry barred the way when Julian, Dick and Anne ran to their cousin's aid. He caught Julian and had him tied up in a trice. His accomplice dealt with Dick in the same way, taking no notice of Anne's fists as she hammered away at his back, sobbing with fury.

George was simply furious too, but it was no good. The boys struggled, but *that* was no good either. The men were too strong for them. Last of all they caught Anne and wrapped a piece of tent canvas around her, till she was all bundled up like an Egyptian mummy. Then they put her on the ground beside her brothers.

'Come on, Gene, let's get moving!' Harry told his companion. 'There's no one else here. We don't want to keep Albert waiting with the boat. Let's get the gold and be off!'

George jumped – as much as she could in her bonds. The gold! So these men were two of the bank robbers – the gangsters who had stolen the ingots!

'And the gold ingots were hidden here on my island the whole time!' she thought. 'Oh no! That really puts the lid on it!'

She saw Harry and Gene go off into the castle. They must have put the gold in one of the cellars. To think the Five had looked everywhere but in the castle itself! George and her cousins were not gagged, but it would be no use for them to shout – they would only have made the gangsters angry with them! George turned her attention to Timmy. Firmly tied to the tree, the poor dog was struggling more feebly now.

'His collar will strangle him!' thought George. 'This is dreadful! Oh, if only I could get one of my hands free!'

Frantically, she started rubbing the rope binding her wrists on the rough bark of the tree. She grazed her skin, but she still went on. Every minute counted!

The boys kept quiet. Anne was crying silently. There was nothing to be heard but poor Timmy's hoarse breathing, the murmur of the sea, and the noise of the night-time creatures. Suddenly, George almost let out a cry of triumph! She had managed to wear away the rope and get one hand free!

## Chapter Six

## THE POLICE STEP IN AGAIN

Putting out her arm and straining downwards, George stretched as far as she possibly could in the bonds tying her to the tree. She could just reach Timmy! She gently pulled the cord's knot around the trunk towards her and carefully undid it with her one hand. Timmy fell on the grass and lay there panting painfully, trying to get his breath back.

Suddenly the ground shook beneath heavy footsteps – the gangsters were returning.

'Ssh, Timmy!' George told her dog, seeing him bravely trying to struggle to his feet. 'Don't move!'

She trembled with fear as she thought that the two men might be coming back to finish Timmy off.

But Harry and Gene had forgotten all about

the children and Timmy! They went straight past, carrying a heavy metal container, and started down the path to the beach.

'They'll be coming back,' Dick whispered. 'There must be at least two more containers like that, to hold all the gold!'

He was right. The gangsters did come back again, but this time the man called Albert replaced Harry. Gene once called him 'Sanderson', so the four cousins knew they had guessed right. These men were the bank robbers, who had come to recover their loot!

At last the containers were all loaded on board the boat which must have been waiting for the men down in the cove, and the children soon heard the faint sound of oars. Obviously the gangsters wanted to get away in silence, so they weren't using a motor boat.

George was busy using her one free hand to undo the rest of the ropes tying her. Then she got her penknife and set her cousins free too.

'Quick!' she whispered. 'Let's follow them - hurry!'

'In our pyjamas?' asked Anne doubtfully. She didn't think that sounded very sensible.

'Who cares?' said Dick. 'They look just like track suits, and they'll keep us warm on a night like this – but we'd better put our sandals on!'

A couple of minutes later Dick and Julian were pushing the rowing boat out, while George finished putting a cold compress round Timmy's poor neck.

'There, there! Good dog! I'll pay them back for this!' she murmured.

Anne, who had very keen eyes, pointed to the gangsters' boat. It was quite a long way out to sea now, and making straight for the mainland.

'Row hard!' George told the boys.

Sitting at the tiller with Timmy beside her, she steered towards the mainland too, never taking her eyes off the other boat, and urging her cousins on in a low voice.

'Faster – but row quietly! We don't want those horrible men to notice that they're being followed!'

Once the gangsters had landed it took them a little while to unload their metal containers, and that gave the Five time to come ashore unnoticed a little farther down the coast.

'Now what are we going to do?' Julian wondered. 'We can't attack those brutes head on – so what?'

'Let's get closer to them,' George decided. 'They must have a car or a van near here. If we could just take its number ...'

Keeping very quiet indeed, the children crept along the road that ran parallel to the beach. Timmy forgot his poor sore throat and followed George in silence too. After a minute or two they stopped. There was a van standing in the road,

'We must call the police – quick!'

Bates, Farley and Sanderson had mocking smiles on their faces.

with no lights on. The bank robbers were just putting their containers full of gold inside.

'Oh, blow!' whispered Dick. 'We're too late! I was planning to let their tyres down. Then we could have –'

'There's no time to waste talking!' George interrupted. 'We must call the police – quick!'

The gangsters were already closing the doors of the van. They got into the front themselves and started the engine, and the van set off along the road going north from Kirrin.

The children ran as fast as their legs would carry them. They knew there was a teashop called the Hawthorn Tea Rooms round the next corner. When they got there, quite out of breath, and roused the lady who ran the tea rooms from her bed, she had some difficulty understanding what they wanted!

'A tele – telepho – pho – telephone!' begged Julian, panting for breath.

At last the children got through to the police station, and Inspector Bond gave orders to put the police on the alert again.

It didn't look as though the Five would get much rest that night! But Anne suggested they could all go to Kirrin Cottage before they did anything else.

'We've all got a change of clothes there,' she said. 'We'll feel better once we're properly dressed – and then we can go to the police station and see what's going on!'

'Well done!' said George admiringly. 'That was very far-sighted of you, Anne! Good for you!'

Anne blushed, pleased by the compliment. It wasn't so very often that George praised her!

The sky was getting pale when the Five arrived at the police station. It would be dawn quite soon. George and her cousins asked the constable on duty if they could wait there for news of what was happening. Timmy was feeling better now, and seemed ready to join the hunt for the three crooks again.

Suddenly the telephone rang. It was Inspector Bond! He said the three men had just been arrested at a road block, and he was bringing them in himself. He was very pleased to hear that George and her cousins were there at the police station, because he said that would allow an immediate confrontation between the children and the men they accused of taking the gold ingots.

'But I don't understand!' said George in surprise, when the constable told them what the Inspector had said. 'Why does the Inspector need *us* to confront the gangsters? I mean, the gold they were carrying in their van is quite enough to prove they're guilty!'

'Ah, that's the point,' said the constable. 'Seems like the gold hasn't been found at all!'

This unexpected announcement hit the children like a thunderbolt! To their dismay, Inspector Bond confirmed the bewildering news himself when he arrived a little later, escorting Bates, Farley and Sanderson. All three men had mocking smiles on their faces.

'I'd like to believe what you young folk said on the phone,' the Inspector told them, 'but I have to face the facts! These fellows certainly *are* the men we suspect of robbing the bank over two years ago, but yet again there's no evidence. We didn't find a single gold ingot in their van.'

'And you've no right to hold us without any grounds!' said Harry Bates. 'We've served our time fair and square for borrowing that *Golden Galleon*! As for tonight, we were just taking a little trip along the coast for the good of our health. It's natural to want some fresh air after you've been in prison, isn't it?'

George was staggered! Dick and Julian were furious too, and even Anne was as cross as she ever could be. The Inspector and the other policemen were looking very disappointed – but the gangsters were on top of the world! There was nothing for it, the police simply had to let them go. And off they went in triumph – while the Five gloomily returned to Kirrin Island.

As the word of the three men was as good as *their* word in the eyes of the law, there was nothing the police could do. But George wasn't giving in yet!

While they were eating a good breakfast of bacon and eggs in the warm sun that shone down on their camp, she told her cousins, 'We know we weren't dreaming! The gold can't be far away. The gangsters must have hidden it once again, but on the mainland this time. So now we must go back to searching the mainland, asking questions, going over the countryside with a fine toothcomb! We'll find it in the end. I'm going to get my own back on those men for what they did to Timmy!'

And the Five went back to their investigations, working really hard at the job. Julian had a map of the area, and he had ruled into squares all the part between the coast and the place where the gangsters' van had been stopped by the police.

'This is where we must search,' he said.

'Three big containers like that wouldn't have been easy to camouflage,' remarked Dick. 'So the hiding place must be quite a big one.'

Each morning, the Five rowed to the mainland, got their bicycles, and followed all the little roads and paths near Kirrin, searching the whole countryside and looking out for any place that might possibly have been used to hide the missing gold ingots.

'We simply must act fast,' George kept saying. 'Bates and his friends may come back for their loot any time now – and I have an idea the police more or less suspect *us* of having made the whole story up! Well, I want to prove we weren't lying as soon as I possibly can!'

## Chapter Seven

## PETE'S HUT

George was rather hoping Timmy would pick up the gangster's scent, but though he sniffed the ground everywhere they went he still hadn't found anything. And they had searched all sorts of places – old buildings, deserted barns, huts in the fields, caves along the rocky part of the coast. It was all very discouraging.

However, one day when the Five stopped for a picnic lunch in the shade of some trees on the outskirts of a little wood, Anne suddenly cried, 'Oh, look, there's Pete! Let's invite him to share our lunch! Poor Pete – I don't suppose he often has a chance to sit down to a good meal like this one Aunt Fanny gave us for our picnic!'

Pete was a simple-minded boy who lived alone in a hut in the wood. No one knew exactly what age he was, and the people of Kirrin village just called him Daft Pete, though in an affectionate way. He lived on the money he earned doing odd jobs. He was honest and willing, and very good with his hands, and everyone in the village liked him.

Anne was a great friend of his too. Whenever she saw him she used to give him some sweets or a cake, because she knew he liked good things to eat.

'Hallo, Pete!' she said kindly. 'Come and share our picnic!'

Pete went over, smiling at all of them, and sat down in front of the tablecloth they had spread on the grass. It was covered with delicious things – sausage rolls, cold chicken drumsticks, tomatoes, fresh fruit and gingerbread. Aunt Fanny had certainly packed up a good lunch for the children!

In her motherly way, Anne loaded a plate with food and handed it to Pete.

'G-good, g-good!' said Pete, who stammered when he spoke. He smiled and patted his stomach.

Seeing him eat with such a good appetite, Julian and Dick smiled too. Even George found herself relaxing and forgot for a moment that they were getting nowhere in their search for the gold. Timmy bounded around the boy, wagging his tail, and Pete, who got on well with the dog, scratched his head for him.

'Well, what are you doing these days, Pete?' asked Dick.

'M-making things,' replied the boy. 'And I've g-got l-lots of m-money too!'

'Oh, jolly good!' said Anne, smiling. 'So you're a rich man now, are you, Pete?'

The boy's eyes began to shine. 'Oh y-yes!' He lowered his voice, and added in a confidential tone, 'I've g-got t-treasure hidden in m-my hut!'

Julian, Dick and Anne smiled, and pretended to believe him. But George didn't laugh. She looked hard at Pete. Suppose – just suppose he was telling the truth?

The children had finished their lunch now, and while Anne packed up the picnic things and Julian shook out the tablecloth, George suddenly rose to her feet.

'Pete,' she said, 'you told us just now you had treasure in your hut. Would you show it to us?'

A wary look came into the boy's eyes. Seeing it, George was quick to reassure him. 'You know us, Pete! You know we're your friends, and we'd never rob you. But I'm so curious – I'd really love to see it!'

Realising what was in her cousin's mind, Anne agreed. 'Oh yes, Pete, *I'd* like to see your treasure too! Will you show it to us?'

She took the boy's hand and led him towards the wood. Pete gave a shy laugh and went with her. George, Julian, Dick and Timmy followed them.

Pete's hut stood in the middle of a little clearing, sheltered by the trees. It had once been a woodcutter's hut, and was made of good stout logs. Pete pushed the door open and proudly invited the children in. George felt her pulse racing. Her intuition told her she was on the trail of the hidden gold at last – and her intuition wasn't wrong!

'N-now!' announced Pete, thrusting out his chest with pride. 'N-now I'll sh-show you m-my t-treasure!'

He went over to a corner of the hut where a pile of dry firewood was stacked. Pushing it away, he brought out a cracked old jar that had been hidden underneath. He picked it up in both hands and triumphantly put it down in front of his visitors. Then he put his hand inside.

It was an exciting moment! George and her cousins held their breath. The jar was far too small to contain all the gold ingots, but if it contained only *one* gold bar then they were on the right track.

'Th-there!'

And Pete proudly produced a copper door knob, an old cigarette lighter, two gilt buttons off a military uniform, and the coloured glass stopper of an old-fashioned bottle!

The children were badly disappointed. How-

Pete's hut stood in the middle of a little clearing, sheltered by the trees.

The children could hardly believe it! Three metal containers lay side by side in a hole under the bed.

ever, they wouldn't have hurt poor Pete's feelings for the world, so they told him how fine his 'treasures' were, and then said goodbye.

Outside the hut, George heaved a gloomy sigh. 'Another disappointment!' she said. 'Not to mention all the time we've lost!'

'Come on, buck up!' said Dick. 'We still have those old lime kilns at Duddington St Mary to explore. Who knows, we might find something there!'

But sad to say, they found nothing at all in the lime kilns – or in the old ruined church where they went exploring next. They went on searching the countryside for two more days, and still they got nowhere.

On the morning of the third day they went to Kirrin village to stock up with provisions for their camp on the island. They usually met Pete there on market day, helping some of the stall-holders to put up their booths or sell their butter and eggs, and it was market day today – but they couldn't see Pete anywhere.

'I wonder if he's ill?' said tender-hearted Anne to herself. She told her cousins about her worries. They were surprised not to see Pete, too. Where could he be? Anne asked the old woman who kept the flower stall.

'Oh,' said the old woman, nodding, 'yes, poor Pete, he's ill! The doctor's been to his hut to give him some medicine, and we take him things to eat, but of course we can't be dropping in to see him all the time, can we?'

Anne's heart was touched. Poor Pete, ill all alone in the middle of the wood!

'We ought to go and see if he needs anything,' she told her brothers and her cousin.

'Yes, let's do that,' George agreed at once. 'We might as well go there as anywhere else – and at least we'll be doing a good deed!'

So the Five took the path to Pete's hut. They found him lying on his straw mattress, a little feverish, but not really too ill.

'Here, Pete!' said Dick 'We've brought you some blackcurrant juice, and some chocolate and cake.'

'It'll help you get better,' Anne assured him. Then, like the good little housewife she was, she saw that the sick boy's bed was very untidy. 'Now then, Pete,' she said, 'let's remake your bed for you. You sit on that stool while we do it!'

A worried look came into the boy's eyes, and he looked as if he were going to object. But then Dick offered him a piece of chocolate, and he clambered out of bed to get it. George and Julian took their chance to shake his blankets out of doors in the fresh air.

'Poor old Pete – he hasn't even got any sheets,' Julian said. 'Still, we can turn the mattress for him!'

The straw mattress lay on the hard mud floor

of the hut – but when George and her cousin bent to pick it up, Pete let out a cry of alarm and rushed to stop them.

'N-no – d-don't t-touch!' he told them.

'What on earth is the matter, old chap?' Dick cried, fending him off. 'Calm down! No one's going to steal your mattress!'

Julian and George had already picked the mattress up – and then they saw what lay underneath, and stood rooted to the spot!

The children could hardly believe it! A hole had been dug in the mud floor underneath Pete's makeshift bed, and three metal containers lay side by side in the hole, with the mattress covering them like a lid!

The discovery left George so breathless that she began to stammer like Pete.

'The g-gold ingots from *The G-golden G-galleon*!'

Pete managed to wriggle out of Dick's grasp and rushed to put the mattress back in place.

'The – the n-nice m-men – they m-made me p-promise not to t-tell! They gave me lots of m-money to look after their th-things – when they c-come b-back they'll b-beat me if they know you've s-seen those b-boxes!'

George and her cousins exchanged meaning glances. They realised that their search had at last been successful, just when they least expected it! The bank robbers must have thought it all out very carefully. Leaving the gold in Pete's hut was a very clever idea! It meant the gangsters were moving their loot about by stages, with the least possible risk to themselves. Only they hadn't foreseen either that Pete would be ill, or that the children would visit him!

At last George got her normal voice back. 'This is wonderful!' she cried. 'We've done it! All we have to do now is tell the police. They'll set a police trap around the hut – and when the gangsters come back they'll be caught red-handed!'

Pete had got back on his mattress and was lying down as if to defend his precious boxes! That was quite all right so far as the Five were concerned! They were already on their way to the door, planning to get to the police station as fast as possible, when furious barking from Timmy stopped them in their tracks.

'I hear voices,' whispered Julian.

But before he had finished speaking the door opened, and three men came in. Bates, Farley and Sanderson! The gangsters looked very angry indeed when they saw the astonished children. "Those darn kids again!' Farley growled.

George held Timmy back. Remembering their last meeting, she was afraid of what the men might do to him! The newcomers looked all round the hut, and when their eyes fell on Pete the poor boy began to tremble with terror. He groaned miserably.

'No, n-no!' he cried, sitting up on his mattress. 'They d-didn't see anything! I d-didn't show th-them the b-boxes, I swear I d-didn't!'

## Chapter Eight

## DIGGING A TUNNEL

Poor Pete! He had given himself away – and the children too! The Five turned and made a dash for the door. They knew that only flight could save them now! But the three men moved faster than they did. With help from Pete, who was obviously so frightened of them that he would do anything they said, they quickly tied the four cousins together with a rope looped several times round their bodies. And they turned an old tub upside down over Timmy to imprison him.

Then, still helped by a terrified Pete, the bank robbers took the metal containers out of the hole and carried them out to a wheelbarrow. It looked as if they were going to take them away on the barrow. They must have a car parked somewhere along the road, not too far off.

George was seething with rage. She found

failure even harder to bear after coming so close to success.

The gangsters came back one last time, pushed Pete inside the hut, and then closed the door. Almost at once, the children heard loud hammer blows outside.

'They're nailing planks over the door to stop us escaping!' Julian exclaimed.

'And they're boarding up the window too!' said George, as the hut's single window was suddenly darkened.

Soon silence fell again. The bank robbers had left. Overcoming her fright, Anne asked Pete to untie her and the others, but he was too upset to understand. He just huddled in a corner muttering meaningless words to himself. However, by dint of wriggling and squirming, the children finally managed to get free of their bonds, and as soon as she could George ran to set Timmy free as well.

'I'm going to pay them back for *that*, too!' she muttered.

While George comforted the crestfallen Timmy, Julian and Dick tried the door and window to see if they could open them, but it was no good. Meanwhile Anne was trying to reassure poor Pete.

'It's all right, Pete,' she told him kindly. 'Those were bad men, but you see, they didn't take your treasure away, did they? It's still here underneath the firewood. And you'll soon be feeling better. When we get out of here we'll ask the doctor to come and see you again.'

'*When* we get out of here!' murmured George, going over to help the boys. 'It won't be as easy as that! Those planks must be firmly nailed in place – we're never going to force the door or the window!'

In the dim light of the hut, the children searched about for some kind of tool to help them break down the door, but all they could find was an old poker which was too thin to be any good as a lever.

'Oh, bother!' cried Dick, angrily throwing it on the ground. 'This thing won't be any good at all for helping us get out!'

'Wait a minute!' said George, picking the poker up again. 'I've got an idea. We can use it to scratch away the earth underneath the door, and when we've made a hole big enough to wriggle through we can get out that way. Prisoners are always escaping by digging tunnels – I've read about it in no end of books!'

'Well, it's worth a try,' Julian agreed.

He picked up the poker and attacked the ground just below the door. It was quite easy to start a hole in the mud floor. Dick and George dug with their hands, and Anne moved the earth as they piled it up, carrying it back into the hut. Suddenly Timmy jumped up and pushed

George aside with his strong head. Then *he* started scratching away as hard as he could with his front paws!

George burst out laughing.

'Well done, Timmy! You got the idea pretty quickly!'

'Woof!' Timmy agreed, without stopping his digging.

'You're the most intelligent dog in the world, aren't you?'

'Woof!' said Timmy with deep conviction, still digging away.

This comical conversation cheered the others up. The children began to laugh, and Pete caught the infection and copied them. Then Timmy realised that something he was doing must have amused them, so *he* started fooling about! He dug frantically for a while, then stopped short, barked, turned round and round on the spot, jumped at one after another of the children, licked their faces, and then went on digging twice as hard as before.

Since he was doing all the work by himself, showering the children with earth as he dug it up, the cousins had nothing to do but stand there laughing. At this rate they were sure they'd soon be free!

However, after Timmy had dug for a few minutes, he suddenly stopped. He wasn't fooling about any more. He came out of the hole and went over to George, looking very miserable.

'What's the matter, Timmy?' Dick asked. 'Are you tired? No wonder, the way you've been digging.'

Intrigued, George knelt down to feel the bottom of the hole.

'Oh no! He's reached rock!' she announced. 'We can't dig any deeper! I can feel solid rock at the bottom of the hole.'

'Just our luck!' exclaimed Julian gloomily.

'Wait a minute!' said George. 'Let's go on digging the tunnel all the same. Even if it's too small for us, it may still be big enough for Timmy to go through!'

'And then what?' said Dick. 'Even if Timmy gets out, *we'll* still be here!'

'Dick, you're not thinking!' Anne interrupted him. She had already seen her cousin's idea. 'We'll give Timmy a message to carry, won't we, George?'

'Yes,' said George. 'I'll tell him to take it straight to Kirrin Cottage, and then I'm sure my father will come to the rescue!'

And everything happened just as George had planned. The clever dog scrambled under the door and out of the hut with the message tied to his collar. He covered the couple of miles which separated the hut from Kirrin Cottage without even stopping for breath.

Aunt Fanny saw him arrive, and spotted the piece of paper tied to his collar. Her heart sank as she read the message. She went straight off to tell her husband. Uncle Quentin telephoned the police at once, jumped into his car, and hurried away with Timmy to free the prisoners.

The police arrived at Pete's hut a moment after Uncle Quentin. Once they were free, the children told the police about their adventure. They were feeling very glum again. They had failed on the very point of recovering the treasure, and they felt really bad about it!

However, Inspector Bond congratulated them warmly on picking up the trail of the stolen gold again. If he had ever doubted that the children were telling the truth about the gold ingots, he didn't now. The sight of the hole under the mattress, Pete's confused explanations, and the fact that they had all been imprisoned in the hut were quite enough to convince him.

It wasn't what the children were really after, but it was some consolation!

'And now we must hurry back to Kirrin Cottage!' said Uncle Quentin firmly. 'Your mother's very worried, George, and I want to set her mind at rest.'

Back at the cottage, the Five went gloomily out to walk in the garden. They didn't want to go back to Kirrin Island before they knew how the police search for the gangsters was getting on.

So they had supper at Kirrin Cottage that evening, and then went to bed.

They were still in low spirits as they all sat round the breakfast table next morning.

'*I* think,' said George, sighing, 'that one of our adventures is going to come to nothing for the very first time ever! We've failed. I feel awful about it!'

The sound of the telephone ringing interrupted her. Uncle Quentin got up to go and answer it, and when he came back his usually serious face was wreathed in smiles.

'Good news!' he told his wife and the children. 'Inspector Bond has just told me the gangsters' car has been found – and so have they!'

George jumped for joy. 'Hurray! We've got them at last!'

'Well – not exactly, I'm afraid. The fact is, Bates and his friends had an accident. They drove their car into a tree, and it was in hospital that the police found them!'

Dick couldn't help laughing. 'Well, it serves them right!' he said. 'Crime doesn't pay!'

'Maybe not, but the bank still hasn't got its gold ingots back,' Uncle Quentin went on. 'Once again they don't seem to have had the gold with them.'

'Oh no!' cried George. 'This really is too bad! It looks as if we'll *never* be able to prove they're guilty!'

'Hurray! We've got them at last!' said George.

'Calm down, George, and listen to the rest of the story. Farley was the worst hurt of the three of them, and he's feverish and raving in delirium. There's been a policeman sitting by his bed to take down everything he says – and without intending to in the least, he's given the truth away in his ravings!'

'My goodness, Uncle Quentin!' exclaimed Anne. 'What did he say?'

'First of all, he admitted that he and his accomplices really did rob the bank two years ago – so that's one thing gained for a start! Then, as far as the police can gather from his incoherent ravings, it was like this –'

'Wait a minute, Father!' George interrupted. 'Let's see if I can guess what happened! I think Bates, who seems to be the gang leader, organised the recovery of the gold bars from *The Golden Galleon* with his accomplices. *That* operation certainly succeeded, as we know! And this is what I think happened next. For some reason – say their car broke down, or something like that – the bank robbers couldn't get away with their loot at once. So they hid it in the cellars of the castle on Kirrin Island, just for the time being. *Then*, when they wanted to come back and fetch it, they had to be very careful, because thanks to us the police were on the alert!'

George had said 'thanks to us' in a tone of simple pride that made her parents smile.

'Good reasoning, George!' said her father. 'Go on!'

'Well, it was at this moment,' George continued, 'that the gangsters had the idea of working by slow stages. That would reduce the risk of being caught. And their idea came off, too, because the first time they were arrested they were empty-handed! But each time they moved the gold, they were taking it a little farther from Kirrin. However, the next move didn't succeed so well!'

'Except,' Dick interrupted, 'that they seem to have hidden the metal containers somewhere else just before they crashed their car! So *that* doesn't get us much farther!'

'I don't agree,' said Julian. 'All we have to do is go back to treasure hunting! And remember, at least we have nothing to fear from the gangsters now!'

'You're right!' cried George, in high spirits again. 'Let's start off straight away!'

Aunt Fanny had just turned on the radio to get the news, and they suddenly heard the newsreader's voice like an echo of George's.

'The bank has asked us to broadcast the following message about the stolen gold ingots. While the bank robbers are now in police custody, the ingots themselves have not yet been recovered, and the men themselves refuse to say where they have hidden their loot. A reward of twenty-five thousand pounds is offered to anyone who finds and returns the gold. The police hunt is still going on.'

'Gosh!' said Dick. 'A reward!'

'I wonder if we can move faster than the police?' said Anne.

'Twenty-five thousand pounds!' said Julian thoughtfully. 'That's a lot of money.'

'And we could do with it, too!' said George, her eyes shining.

'George, whatever do you mean?' asked Aunt Fanny, rather shocked to hear her daughter sound so greedy.

'Oh, Mother, it would be wonderful! It's poor Pete I'm thinking of – he lives in such a miserable little hut, and if we earned the reward we could buy him a proper little house and furnish it nicely. What do you think?' she asked the others.

'A very good idea,' said Julian.

'Brilliant!' cried Dick.

'Marvellous!' said Anne.

'Woof!' finished Timmy.

Uncle Quentin and Aunt Fanny were very pleased to see how generous George and her cousins were. How nice it would be if they *could* earn that reward!

## Chapter Nine

## TREASURE HUNTING

The children were full of enthusiasm again as they drew up plans for their treasure hunt. However, before they started out they decided to go and see Pete. They wanted to make sure their friend was getting better and hadn't been too badly upset by what happened the day before.

'We won't mention our plans about a house for him, of course,' Julian warned the others as they cycled towards the little wood. 'Poor Pete would be so disappointed if we failed.'

'We won't fail!' said George confidently.

They found that Pete was very much better when they reached his hut. He was out of bed and looking at his 'treasures'. They had all brought presents for him. Dick gave him a pretty glass marble, Anne had some barley sugar, Julian gave him a whistle, and George had brought an old watch of Uncle Quentin's which still worked. Pete was delighted! Quite beside himself with joy, he started dancing around the room. Timmy got all excited too, and went leaping about and barking loudly. The pair of them fooled about for quite a while, much to the amusement of the four cousins.

Suddenly Timmy stopped pirouetting and dropped back on all-fours. The hair on his back was bristling, and he let out a low growl. Then he breathed very hard and sneezed. George ran forward. Her dog had stopped to look at a dirty red and white handkerchief.

'It's Bates's handkerchief!' cried Dick. 'I saw him mopping his forehead with it when they were taking the metal containers out of the hut. He must have dropped it!'

'Good!' said George. 'I bet my dog can get on the bank robbers' trail now!'

'Get on the bank robbers' trail?' asked Julian. 'But we don't need to do that – we know where they are all right! They're in prison!'

'You don't understand,' replied George impatiently. 'I didn't say Timmy would find the bank robbers – I said he'd get on their trail!'

'I don't see any difference,' Julian objected.

'Oh, but there *is* a difference,' said Dick. 'George means that if we follow the gangsters' trail from this hut we ought to end up at the spot where they stopped to hide the gold ingots.'

'Wonderful!' exclaimed Anne enthusiastically.

'Just a minute,' said Julian. 'Aren't you all forgetting that Bates and his accomplices didn't leave on foot? They were in a car – the one they crashed. So how can Timmy follow their trail?'

'Woof!' said Timmy firmly. 'Woof, woof!'

'I think Timmy's just answered your question!' said George, laughing. 'He's reminding you that the gangsters *started* from here on foot, pushing a wheelbarrow. Well, the place where they stopped to load the gold into their car will be our first clue, and after that –'

'Anyway, don't let's waste any more time talking!' Dick said. 'Come on, Tim, old boy! Have a good sniff at the delicious scent of this pretty hanky, and try not to faint away!'

Timmy gravely sniffed the dirty handkerchief they held out to him and then trotted to the doorway, wagging his tail. All they had to do was follow him!

Leaving Pete gazing delightedly at his new 'treasures', the children hurried off after the dog, their hearts full of hope. Timmy went on at a leisurely pace, nose close to the ground, taking great care not to go too fast for his companions.

The dog followed the woodland path which led to the main road for quite a way. Julian still wasn't very hopeful, and he expressed his doubts to the others again.

'We can see the marks the wheels of the barrow left on this path all right – but the road certainly won't show the traces of the car's tyres!'

'Let's wait and see what happens!' said George.

At last Timmy reached the road. Then he raised his nose, sniffed the air, and let out a very promising "Woof!' After that he crossed the road and plunged into the undergrowth on the other side.

The four cousins looked at each other in surprise.

'Well, who'd have thought it?' said Dick. 'Either old Timmy's made a mistake, or the gangsters didn't leave by car at all!'

'Timmy *never* makes mistakes!' said George firmly.

'Quick!' cried Anne. 'Let's follow him!'

The children walked on for quite a long way, following the dog. At last Timmy came to an open space. 'Why, it's the Duddington diggings!' George and her cousins exclaimed in chorus.

This was the name the local people gave to the archaeological excavations at the Abbey of Duddington St James, an old monastery which had been built in the Middle Ages on the site of an even older village. A party of archaeologists had begun digging up the remains, but then their funds ran out, and now the Abbey was deserted.

Without the slightest hesitation, Timmy made for the cloister garden of the Abbey, and the children hurried after him.

The garden, which stood in the middle of the old cloisters, was a real mess! The people doing the digging work for the archaeologists had flung up the soil and dug deep trenches. They had found some old medieval tombs in the holes they dug, and now the old tombs, with their stone lids, were all standing in a corner of the cloisters.

His nose still close to the ground, Timmy went over to one of the tombs and sniffed it with great interest.

'Woof!' he said, turning to George.

'Timmy, are you sure?' she asked breathlessly.

'Woof!' repeated Timmy.

The boys came forward, and both pushing at it together they managed to lift the heavy, moss-grown lid. George and Anne leaned over to look inside. There was a big bag made of stout canvas inside the old tomb.

Julian immediately checked to see what was inside the canvas bag. 'Hurray! The gold ingots at last!' he cried.

'Look Timmy's sniffing at the tomb next to it now,' said Anne.

They found two more canvas bags in the next two tombs. They seemed to be holding everything that had been inside those three metal

'Hurray! The gold ingots at last!' cried Julian.

They heard the sound of a very noisy car engine.

containers. At long last, the Five had found the stolen gold again!

Simply delighted, the children took hands to dance around the old stone tombs – and Timmy joined in too!

'All we need is some music to dance to!' said Dick cheerfully, taking his little radio out of his pocket.

But it wasn't music he got when he switched it on! All at once, they heard the newsreader's voice again.

'Two of the recently arrested bank robbers, Bates and Sanderson, have managed to escape from the prison hospital, and have not yet been traced by the police ...'

'Oh, good gracious!' cried Anne, turning pale. 'The first thing they'll do if they're free is come straight here to look for the gold!'

It was a very tense moment. Anne, terrified, looked around as if she expected to see the two bank robbers appear at any moment. Dick, looking rather worried too, had planted himself in front of the bags of gold as if to protect them. Julian, who was determined not to panic, was trying to think. George, whose courage and coolness seldom failed her even in a very tight corner, said nothing at all. But she too was thinking hard, frowning with the effort, before she came to a decision. Timmy waited in silence, his eyes fixed on his mistress.

'We mustn't panic,' she said at last. 'Let's look at the whole situation. The gold is here – thanks to Timmy, we've found it. And we've earned the reward offered by the bank! Well – we don't want the gangsters snatching their loot from under our very noses the way they've done twice already!'

'That's all right as far as it goes,' said Dick, 'but they may turn up any moment now, and we know they're too strong for us, so *how* do you suggest we stop them going off with the gold ingots?'

'What we need,' said Julian thoughtfully, 'is some way of getting the ingots away at once.'

'But we can't,' said Anne. 'It would take some time for anyone to run to Duddington St James village and get someone to come with a car!'

'You're right,' George agreed. 'So I can see only one thing to do. As the gold is too heavy for us to carry, we must hide it here! And then we'll come back for it later – with my father and the police.'

'We move it out of these old tombs, you mean?' said Dick. 'Good idea – but *where* shall we hide it?'

George didn't hesitate for a moment. 'Quick – we'll drag the canvas bags over to the nearest trench!' she said. 'We can cover them up with earth, and the gangsters will never guess the loot is here within their reach!'

Her cousins agreed that that was a good idea.

'Right – to work!' said Julian.

The four children had soon dragged the bags over to the side of one of the deep trenches. They pushed them in – and then all they had to do was cover them up with some of the earth piled up at the side of the trench. Finally they made sure they had removed all traces of what they had been doing. The whole operation took only a few minutes.

'We still have to get the lids back on the three old tombs,' said George.

'Do let's hurry!' begged Anne. 'I don't like this at all.'

'Neither do I,' Julian admitted. 'The radio didn't say just *when* the gangsters escaped – but the town where they were in prison hospital isn't far away. It wouldn't take them long to get here if they stole a car.'

'All the same, they have to keep under cover, so that may delay them,' Dick pointed out.

Soon the three heavy lids were back on the old medieval tombs, and no one would ever have guessed that they had been opened.

'Now let's hurry back to the village!' said George.

Then something odd happened. Just as she started off along the path to the village, with the others ready to follow her, Timmy barred her way, snapping at her ankle and growling quietly.

George stopped, astonished. 'Timmy, what–

ever *are* you doing? Why won't you let me by?'

Timmy took George's hand in his mouth, gently closed his jaws over it, and tried to pull her back.

'Timmy doesn't seem to want us to go to the village,' said Dick in surprise.

Then Timmy made as if to go in the opposite direction, and turned his head back to see if his little mistress was following.

'Let's see what he wants,' said George.

As soon as Timmy realised that the children had decided to follow him, he dashed off and disappeared behind a thick bush. Intrigued, the four cousins began to run, and they found Timmy sitting behind the bush waiting for them. At the same moment they heard the sound of a very noisy car engine.

'Someone's coming up from the village,' said Julian. 'In what sounds like a real old Tin Lizzie! Timmy heard it before we did!'

'But why did he stop us going to meet it?' asked Anne. 'Somebody in a car – *any* sort of car! – is just what we need!'

'I'm sure dear old Tim had his reasons,' murmured George, peering through the leaves.

Dick looked too, and then he whistled.

'I say! It's Bates and Sanderson!'

*Chapter Ten*

## UP TO THE BELFRY

Sure enough it was the two gangsters arriving at the archaeological diggings in a very noisy old van.

'All they could find to take their gold ingots away in, I suppose,' whispered Julian.

'What gold ingots?' Dick whispered back, in fits of suppressed laughter. 'I bet you anything they won't find so much as a grain of medieval gold in those old tombs!'

'Ssh!' George hissed at her cousins. 'This is no time for silly jokes! We just avoided running straight into them, thanks to Timmy – that would have been awful! However, when they find their loot has disappeared they're sure to have a good search for it – and what they'll find is *us*, if we don't hurry to get away!'

'But where can we go?' asked Anne anxiously.

George pointed to the Abbey chapel.

'Let's hide up in the belfry there!' she suggested. 'I think it should be safe enough. It would be really bad luck if they decided to go up into that tower.'

'What's more, we'll be able to see what they're doing,' said Julian.

Silently, the Five crept through the ruins of the Abbey towards the chapel. They slipped in, and then started climbing the spiral staircase which led up the belfry. The chapel was the only part of the Abbey which had been completely restored, and when they reached the top of the stairs the children saw a very fine bronze bell. Cautiously, Dick stuck his head out of a little window.

'Yes, I can see them,' he told the others in a low voice. 'They're just lifting the lid of the first tomb – go on, then! Yo-heave-ho! Watch for the birdie!'

George and Julian could hardly help laughing at Dick's fun, but Anne was too worried even to smile. The gangsters were going to be furious when they found their gold was gone!

Down below, the two men had just lifted the lid of the first stone tomb, and they both leaned over the edge. For a moment, nothing at all happened. There was total silence. Then, suddenly, the gangsters exploded with rage.

The children could hear their voices.

'It's impossible!' shouted Bates. 'The gold can't have vanished into thin air! Oh, if I could just get hold of whoever took it!'

'Perhaps we're looking in the wrong tomb?' said Sanderson, recovering from the worst of the shock.

'Let's see!'

Working feverishly, the two men took off the lids of all the other stone tombs – and each time they lifted one their shouts of fury made poor Anne tremble. Finally, the gangsters could no longer doubt it – the gold ingots really *had* disappeared!

'Robbed! We've been robbed!' cried Bates, quite forgetting that *he* was the robber himself in the first place. 'Who can have done it?'

'I bet it was those perishing kids!' said Sanderson. 'You know – the ones who keep getting under our feet all the time! First they nearly snapped up the gold from the wreck itself, then they gave us trouble on that island, and finally they tracked us down to Pete's hut! They're a bright bunch all right!'

'You're right. I can't think of anyone else who could have beaten us to it – but how could they have got the gold away?'

'Yes, that's odd. And surely if they'd found the ingots the police would know? There'd have been a police trap waiting for us here – but there isn't!

'May be the kids just kept the treasure for themselves?' suggested Bates. 'Oh, if I could only get my hands on them!'

At that moment a dreadful howl broke the silence. By mistake, Dick had just trodden on Timmy's paw, and the poor dog yowled in pain. 'OOOOWWW!'

Transfixed by terror, the children held their breath. Timmy was waving his bruised paw in the air apologetically, but the damage had been done! His howl of pain had drawn the attention of the gangsters to the belfry.

'Hear that?' Sanderson asked Bates.

'Of course I did! I'm not deaf! Sounded as if it came from up there.'

'It sound like a dog, too. What do you bet it's the dog that goes about with those kids? The little scallywags are hiding up there with our gold!'

'Oh, come on! They could never have got it up the tower.'

'Then they've hidden it in the chapel! Come along – I'm sure I'm right!'

The two men raced to the chapel. Anne was shaking all over. 'Oh, my goodness!' she breathed. 'We're done for!'

'Not yet!' Julian told her. 'If we can just keep our heads we may be able to escape them.'

'How?' asked Dick.

'Down the bell-rope!'

'I shall _never_ abandon Timmy,' George said fiercely.

'Why, yes!' cried Dick, rushing to the belfry door and bolting it. 'Once the gangsters arrive and try to force this door, we'll slide down the bell-rope to the bottom of the tower and run off. And by the time the men come down again we'll be well away!'

'Good thinking, Dick. You see my idea!'

'And a jolly good idea it is too, Ju!' said George. 'Anne, I hope you won't be frightened. Now – we must all tear our handkerchiefs in two and wrap them round our hands, to protect our palms from getting grazed by the rope!'

But Julian saw that George wasn't doing the same at the rest of them. He was going to ask her why not, but the arrival of the bank robbers at the top of the stairs prevented him.

Timmy barked.

'Open up!' ordered Bates, shaking the door. 'I can hear you kids in there! Get a move on – open up!'

'Hurry!' George whispered to her cousins. 'Go on – you first, Julian, and then you follow directly after him, Anne. Then it will be Dick's turn. Quick – you must run for help!'

'But aren't you coming with us, George?' cried Dick.

George firmly shook her head.

'No,' she said, 'Timmy can't climb down a rope, so I must stay with him. The two of us will try to keep the gangsters here until you can send reinforcements.'

'Oh, George!' cried Anne in her turn. 'Do come – *please*!'

'No, it's no use trying to persuade me. Hurry up, all of you!'

Blows were hammering on the door. It wasn't very strong, and it could only be a matter of time before Bates and Sanderson broke it down. There wasn't a moment to be lost!

Julian took George's arm.

'George, your life could be in danger!' he said. 'I'm very fond of Timmy, as you know, but your safety comes before his!'

George shook his hand off quite roughly.

'I shall *never* abandon Timmy!' she said fiercely. 'And I'm not afraid of the gangsters! Why don't you think of Anne's safety instead of mine?'

She firmly pushed Julian towards the square opening in the floor of the belfry. A stout rope passed through it. This was the bell-pull which enabled the bellringers to ring the bell from the bottom of the belfry tower.

Realising that every moment they wasted arguing endangered their chances, Julian gave in. He grasped the rope firmly in both hands and slid down it to the ground. Of course that made the bell itself ring out!

'Help!' said Dick. 'The noise will give us away!'

'No, it won't!' replied George. 'The gangsters know we're here already – they'll just think we're ringing the bell to try to summon help! And they'll guess that even if the sound *is* heard, no one will take much notice – how's anyone to know what's going on here?'

She pushed Anne towards the square opening.

'Your turn now, Anne! Hold tight to the rope and let yourself slide down it. Close your eyes if you're frightened. Julian will catch you at the bottom.'

The bell was making a jangling and very unmelodious sound. It had just finished clanging when Dick, in his turn, reluctantly disappeared through the opening.

Once again the clapper moved violently for a few moments, and then the echoes died away. George looked through the little belfry window and saw her cousins running for the village as fast as they could go. They had got safely away!

But now the brave girl was left to face the bank robbers alone, with her faithful dog Timmy!

One last blow shook the door, and then it flew open. The gangsters rushed into the belfry.

Seeing George and her dog standing there, the two men stopped in surprise.

'There's only the one lad – the little girl, I mean!' said Bates, remembering the mistake he had made about George earlier, on Kirrin Island. 'Where did the other three go?'

'They decided they weren't too keen on your company!' said George coolly. 'So they didn't wait for you. You can always try running after them!'

'This is too much!' exploded Sanderson. He just couldn't get over it! 'The kids got away through that hole! And I thought they were only ringing the bell to rouse the villagers!'

Bates was looking dangerous. He went over to George, who was holding back Timmy – who wanted to spring at the crooks, but she was afraid of what might happen to him. 'So you and your little friends pinched our gold, eh?' he shouted. 'Go on, you might as well admit it! The rest of 'em are too far off for us to catch them now, but you're our prisoner. And you're going to tell us where you hid the gold ingots! Better be quick about it – we want to be well away from here when the police arrive!'

George merely crossed her arms and looked defiantly at the gangsters.

'I've nothing to say to you,' she told them. 'That gold isn't yours, and it must go back to the bank.'

Timmy was snarling in a low tone, ready to leap at his mistress's enemies the moment she gave him the word. But Bates did not seem worried by that. He kept advancing on George.

She didn't know if the man was armed or not – and if he did have a gun, she was afraid he might shoot her beloved dog. So she ordered him, 'Sit, Timmy! Sit!'

Sanderson, the other man, laughed unpleasantly. 'So you've seen sense, little girl! Well, don't keep us waiting. Tell us what we want to know! If you don't ...'

He had taken a knife out of his pocket and was waving it about in a threatening way. George laughed defiantly.

'I'm not saying anything!' she said scornfully. 'And if you cut my throat – well, I'll be saying even less, won't I?'

## Chapter Eleven

### DOWN THE WELL

Meanwhile Julian, Dick and Anne had run out of breath and were slowing down. They were right in the middle of the wood now, and they realised no one was following them.

'But George is in danger!' said Julian. He was very worried. 'You know, we *can't* just leave her there facing those men!'

'No, we can't,' Dick agreed. 'Let's go back and help her. We'll come up on the gangsters from behind – there are only two of them now, and if we take them by surprise we may be able to overpower them.'

'But if we don't we'll *all* be in trouble! No, I know what we'll do. Anne, you run on through the wood and fetch help, and meanwhile Julian and I will go back to the belfry.'

'But suppose I lose my way on my own?'

faltered Anne. 'I don't know this wood very well.'

Just then, two children who seemed to be out picking blackberries, a boy and a girl, came round a bush. Julian called out to them.

'I say – you two! Would you mind helping us?'

The boy came over to him with a smile. He had a nice face.

'Help you? Yes, of course we will,' he said. 'My name's Jimmy, and this is my cousin Catherine. Wht do you want us to do?'

'Would you take my sister Anne to the police station in Duddington St James? She'll tell you what it's all about on the way. We're in a dreadful hurry!'

'Right,' said Jimmy. 'Come along, Anne!'

With a last look back at her brothers, Anne followed the two children. Julian turned to Dick.

'Well, it's up to us now, old chap! Let's go back to help George!'

But as the two boys set off at a run they almost collided with Pete. He came running up looking very scared.

'The b-b-bell!' stammered the boy. 'The b-bell rang!'

Dick suddenly had a brilliant idea.

'Listen, Pete!' he said. 'The bad men are in the belfry there! They're going to hurt George – you remember George, who gave you a lovely watch?'

'Oh, yes – I l-like G-george!'

'Well, she's in danger. Would you like to help us rescue her?'

'Yes, yes! P-pete will help!'

Dick had already drawn up a plan. He quickly explained it to Pete, who seemed to understand what he was to do. When the three boys came within sight of the bell tower, Julian and Dick managed to get into the chapel without being seen. Then Pete ran round outside the bell tower, stood at the bottom, and called out very loud.

'Hey! Up th-there! Y-you, up there!'

Bates stopped advancing on George and went to the window to look out. Sanderson instinctively lowered his knife and turned to the window as well. Quick as a flash, George made a dash for the spiral staircase, followed by Timmy. Half-way down she met her cousins coming up, armed with some excavating tools they had found in a corner.

'Oh, good!' cried Dick, seeing George. 'We hoped you'd manage to get away if we created a distraction – well, come on, let's run for it!'

But the gangsters had only been distracted for a moment by Pete's shouting. They soon pulled themselves together, and came after the children!

George and the boys got out of the tower ahead of them, and ran to hide in the wood with Pete – but the gangsters could run very fast, and there was a desperate chase through the trees! Julian, Dick and George used all sorts of tricks to throw their pursuers off, but none of them worked. The terrified Pete followed them like a shadow.

Gradually, the children realised they would have to stand and face the bank robbers. Their frantic chase had brought them back to the Abbey garden, and they came to an old well where the monks once used to draw their water.

Dick and Julian stopped here, brandishing the spade and pick they had found. George picked up a branch, which she was going to use as a club. Timmy growled and showed his teeth. Pete was howling like a factory siren!

'Got 'em!' shouted Bates.

He was an athletically built man, and wasn't afraid of a few children – and anyway, his rage re-doubled his strength. He lunged forward. George ducked away to avoid a collision – and at the same moment Dick put out a leg and tripped the gangster up. Bates certainly wasn't expecting anything like that! He lost his balance and fell head first down the well – the ruinous little wall surrounding it was hardly above ground level.

Seeing the more dangerous of their enemies disappear, Julian was quick to react. He flung himself on Sanderson, and Timmy immediately followed suit. The gangster fought back. He grabbed Julian by the throat, taking no notice of Timmy, who was hanging on to his jacket.

And then, following the dog's example, Pete took a hand in things. He clung to one of the

Dick put out a leg and tripped the gangster up.

The children were letting him down to join his accomplice.

117

gangster's arms, while Timmy took advantage of his opportunity to snap at the man's heels. Helpless for the moment, Sanderson shouted to Bates to come and help him.

That was just too bad, because Bates was at the bottom of the well, and *he* needed help himself! Sanderson's shout only attracted the attention of George and Dick, who were leaning over the side of the well. They both turned and made for the gangster – and five minutes later the children had him tied to the end of the chain that went down the well, and were letting him down to join his accomplice.

After that, Dick calmly unhooked the chain and dropped the whole thing down the well after them!

'You should be thankful the well's dry at the moment!' he told the gangsters. 'Just wait patiently. I'm sure the police will be delighted to help you out!'

George and her cousins had won the battle! They felt very pleased with themselves. It was a real victory – not only had they got back the gold ingots stolen by the bank robbers, they had taken the men prisoner too! All they had to do now was hand them over to the police and give the gold back to the bank.

Kneeling on the grass, George kissed Timmy's nose. 'Good, *good* dog!' she told him. 'You did very well. I'm so proud of you!'

Julian and Dick were congratulating Pete.

'You were very brave, Pete! You helped us no end! But don't worry, you'll get your reward!'

Beaming, he started to chuckle and then roar with laughter.

The children didn't have to mount guard for long over the well and the trench where the gold lay hidden. Anne, guided by Jimmy and Catherine, had alerted the police at the local station as fast as she could. She soon came back with several policemen. They had been in touch with the Kirrin police, and Inspector Bond and his men arrived on the scene at almost the same moment as the policemen from Duddington St James.

George was very happy to see the two parties of policemen.

'Thank you for coming to help us,' she told them. 'And thank *you* for being so quick, Anne. Well, the fun's all over,' she told Inspector Bond, with a big grin, 'but you can take delivery of the goods now!'

'What goods?' asked Inspector Bond, rather baffled, looking round in surprise. 'I thought we'd been called to come and overpower the bank robbers, but – '

'But we've already done that!' Dick interrupted. 'If you want to put the handcuffs on them, all you have to do is fish them out of that old well!'

'And as for the gold ingots,' said Julian, straight-faced, 'you'll find them covered by some earth in the trench over there!'

'Good Lord!' said the Inspector, staggered. 'You kids have certainly been busy!'

He was so surprised that that was all he could say at first! It wasn't until a little later that he thought of congratulating the Five – and so did the other policemen.

The day before they went back to school for the autumn term was a very special day for the Five. Now that the gangsters had been captured, and the gold ingots were back in the bank, they had been given the promised reward. They had been looking over special several cottages before they found one which they thought would do for Pete. Aunt Fanny went house-hunting with them to give advice.

On the morning of the great day they set off cheerfully to instal Pete in his new home. They went to pick him up at his hut and took him to Kirrin village.

A little white cottage with a green door stood by the roadside, with a pretty garden full of flowers in front of it. Aunt Fanny and Uncle Quentin had furnished it inside themselves.

George took Pete's hand and led him in, and Anne happily invited him to look round the little place.

'This is your new home now, Pete!' George told him. 'Old Mr Johnson, your next-door neighbour, has promised to find you regular work, and Mrs Johnson will see you get your meals. How about that?'

Pete clapped his hands for joy. He went from room to room, thanking his friends, so happy he almost didn't stammer when he talked any more!

Leaving him to settle into his new home, the children mounted their bicycles and rode back to Kirrin Cottage with Timmy bounding alongside them.

'Back to school tomorrow!' sighed Dick. 'The holidays are over!'

'But what wonderful holidays they've been!' Anne reminded him.

'You're right, Anne!' said Julian. 'Our adventure had a disappointing start, but then it turned out to be a very fine one indeed! *And* we've been able to make Pete happy.'

'The Five come out on top yet again!' cried George. 'We're pretty good detectives, aren't we, Timmy?'

'Woof, woof!' said Timmy.

# ENID BLYTON

## THE FAMOUS FIVE AND THE STATELY HOMES GANG

The Five are pleased to be spending another holiday at Kirrin Cottage, the scene of many of their adventures. And this holiday proves to be as exciting as all the others, from the moment they set off on their shiny new bicycles!

**KNIGHT BOOKS**

**ENID BLYTON**

## THE FAMOUS FIVE AND THE MYSTERY OF THE EMERALDS

A summer holiday camping on Kirrin Island is the prospect in store for the Five, and they're eagerly looking forward to exploring the island.

But when George overhears a couple of crooks planning a jewel robbery, the Famous Five set off on a dangerous and thrilling trail.

**KNIGHT BOOKS**

# ENID BLYTON

## THE FAMOUS FIVE AND THE MISSING CHEETAH

Arriving for two weeks' stay at Big Hollow, the children are delighted to discover that Tinker has a new friend – a cheetah!

But twenty-four hours later, Attila the cheetah has been kidnapped, and his abductors threaten to shoot him unless they're given the formula for a new, top-secret fuel.

**KNIGHT BOOKS**

# ENID BLYTON

## THE FAMOUS FIVE GO ON TELEVISION

A holiday treat is even more exciting than
expected when the Five are invited to play
themselves in a television series.

Shooting is disturbed, however, by some
sudden and mysterious disappearances. The
children suspect that a kidnapper is at work.
But who, and why?

**KNIGHT BOOKS**

**ENID BLYTON**

**THE FAMOUS FIVE VERSUS
THE BLACK MASK**

A Mediterranean cruise on the liner North
Wind is an exciting prospect for the Five and
their friend Tinker.

Then a series of thefts confirms a rumour
that the famous international criminal, the
Blask Mask, is on board! Who, out of all the
innocent-looking passengers, can the thief
be? The children are determined to find out
before the end of the holiday!

**KNIGHT BOOKS**

A complete list of the FAMOUS FIVE
ADVENTURES by Enid Blyton:

**KNIGHT BOOKS**

More exciting adventures from Knight Books

## ENID BLYTON

☐ 26525 6  THE FAMOUS FIVE AND THE
STATELY HOMES GANG  75p
☐ 26524 8  THE FAMOUS FIVE AND THE
MYSTERY OF THE
EMERALDS  75p
☐ 27248 1  THE FAMOUS FIVE AND THE
MISSING CHEETAH  75p
☐ 27247 3  THE FAMOUS FIVE GO ON
TELEVISION  75p
☐ 27864 1  THE FAMOUS FIVE VERSUS
THE BLACK MASK  85p